For Imani Margaret Phillips, Mikah Taylor Harris, and Pe'Tehn Raighn-Ken Jackson

—U.E.P.

I dedicate this book to Luke, Chloe, McKenna, and McKhai for making this project the best it could be, and to all the children the world over with the knowledge that you are tomorrow's promise.

—B.C.

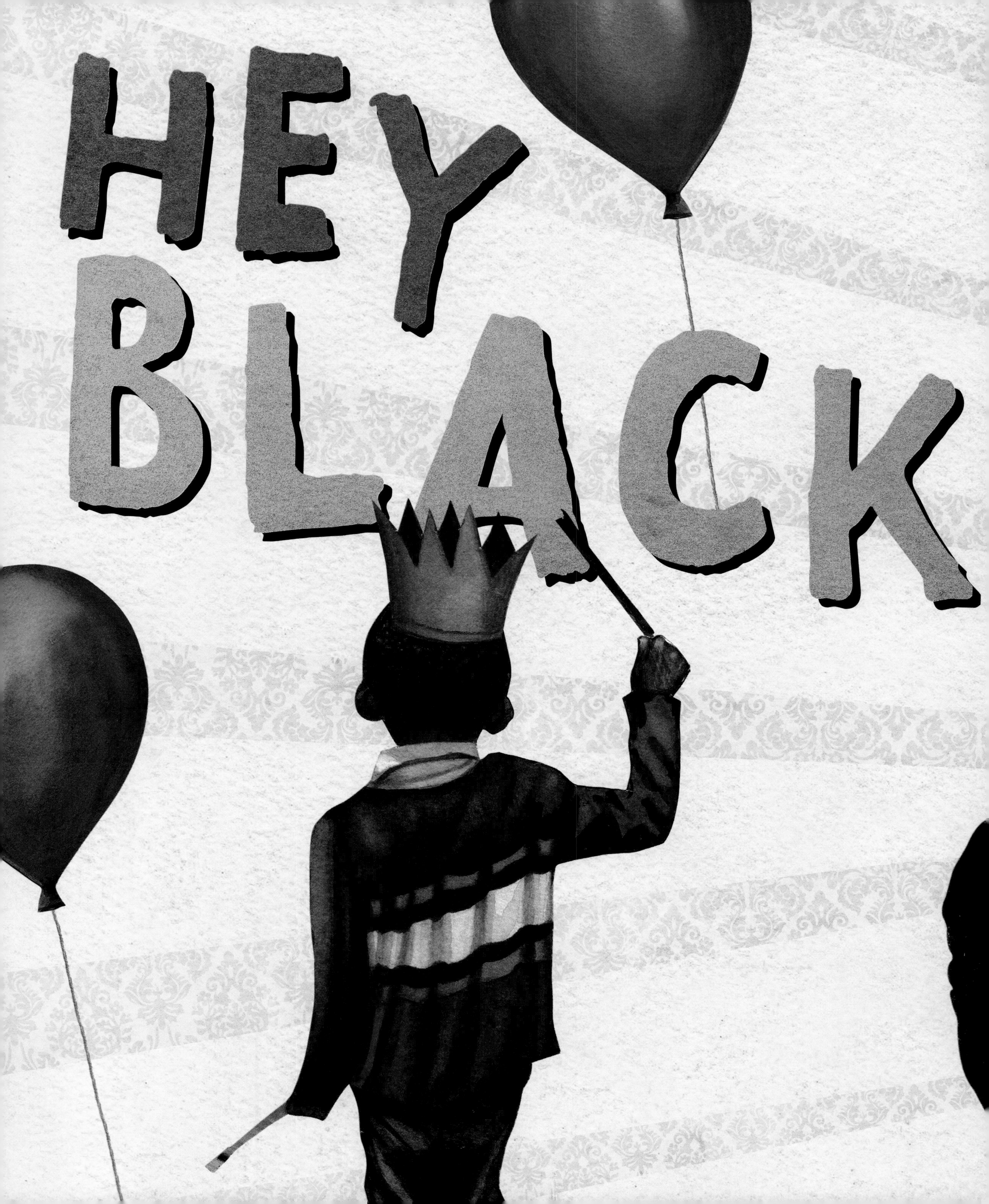
HEY
BLACK

CHILD

by
USENI EUGENE
PERKINS

illustrated by
BRYAN COLLIER

SCHOLASTIC INC.

Hey Black Child

Do you know who you are

Who you **REALLY ARE**

Do you know you can be
What you want to be
If you try to be
What you **CAN BE**

Hey Black Child

Do you know where you are going
Where you are REALLY GOING

10

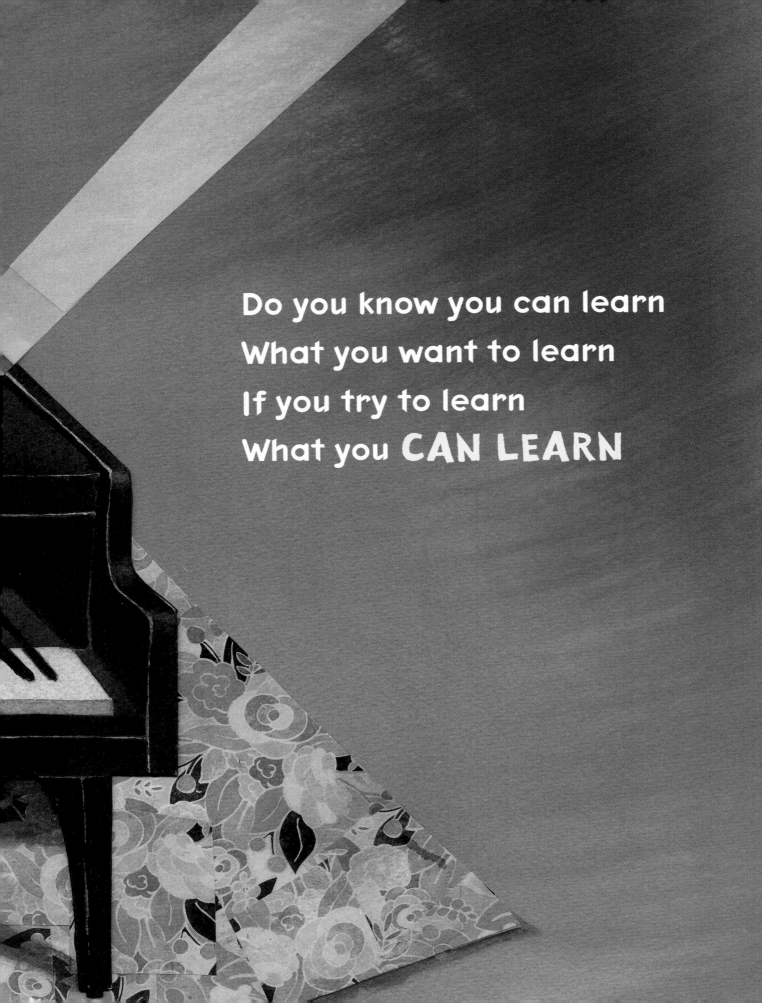

Do you know you can learn
What you want to learn
If you try to learn
What you **CAN LEARN**

Hey Black Child

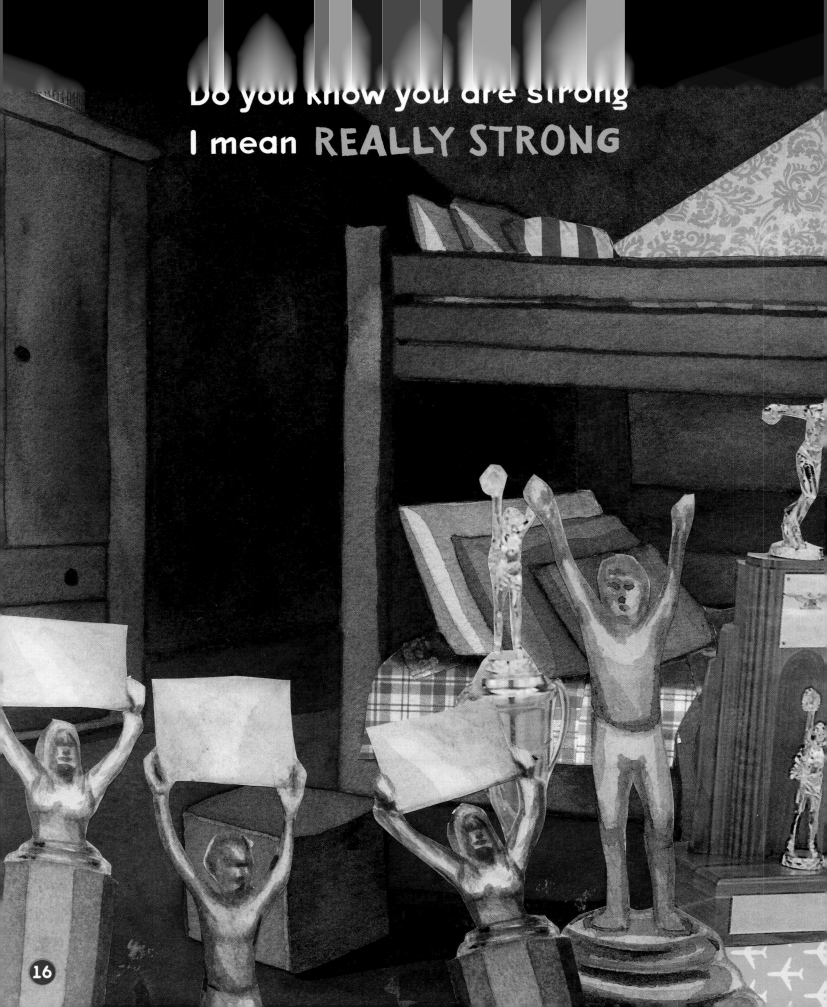

Do you know you are strong
I mean REALLY STRONG

Do you know you can do
What you want to do
If you try to do
What you **CAN DO**

Hey Black Child

Be what you CAN BE

Learn what you

MUST LEARN

Do what you CAN DO

And tomorrow

YOUR NATION

WILL BE WHAT YOU

WANT IT TO BE

AUTHOR'S NOTE

I feel truly blessed to have Little, Brown Books for Young Readers publish my poem "Hey Black Child," illustrated by award-winning artist Bryan Collier. I first wrote this poem in 1975 as the closing song for my children's musical, *Black Fairy and Other Plays*, which has been performed in theaters across the United States. In *Black Fairy*, the main character named Johnny has low self-esteem and must realize his potential to achieve whatever he chooses to be. To help Johnny, the Black Fairy introduces him to her friend Black Bird, and together they meet Queen Mother, the personification of Africa. The four take a journey through history so that Johnny can learn about the many accomplishments black people have given to humankind.

There is an African proverb that states, "Children are the reward of life." This couldn't be more apparent to me by my poem's reception. Since its inception, "Hey Black Child" has been recited and enjoyed by children of all ages across America at various programs and dramatic readings.

However, over the years, "Hey Black Child" has been incorrectly attributed to the great Harlem Renaissance poet Countee Cullen and even to Maya Angelou. I'm honored that my poem has been associated with these two gifted writers, but I'm glad that the world can now learn about the poem's true roots.

I wrote "Hey Black Child" because I wanted to inspire and motivate all black children to achieve their God-given potential, regardless of the challenges they face in life. This is especially true for some black children, who often feel discouraged due to circumstances beyond their control. However, when given the opportunity, resources, and love, black children can achieve heights that are as majestic as the ancient pyramids of Egypt, which were built by their venerable ancestors.

Finally, I hope and pray this book will bring joy and inspiration to all black children and will help give them pride and fortitude in their lives.

—U.E.P.

ILLUSTRATOR'S NOTE

Hey *Black Child* is an ode to young black children that inspires and celebrates their lives. The children throughout discover their own worth and ability to the magical words of Useni Eugene Perkins. This was a moving project where I wanted to capture the inspirational words and touching, powerful moments by showing present-day children, their future accomplishments, and the past lives that have helped us all reach our true potential. This subtheme starts by showing African royalty, before showing the civil rights movement and finally showing modern-day protests such as those for Black Lives Matter.

The art for this book was done in watercolor and collage. Collage works well to show the connections between each character, page, and story, with themes (such as rays of light and balloons) following throughout the book, and also allows the realistic images of actual children and photographs of the men and women, such as Dr. Martin Luther King Jr., who have allowed us to stand on the shoulders of giants.

—B.C.